Mango
moon

Diane de Anda

ILLUSTRATED BY
Sue Cornelison

ALBERT WHITMAN & CO.
CHICAGO, ILLINOIS

*T*here's a full moon out tonight.

Papi called it a mango moon the last
night we stood on the porch together.
We watched the bright orange ball,
the color of the slice of mango in
my hand, rise in the sky.

The chill catches my shoulder without Papi's
arm around me to keep me warm. But I stay
anyway, because this will be the last night
I will welcome the moon from my porch.

Everything changed the day they came to Papi's work and took him away. Mama picked us up from school with her eyes all red. "Maricela and Manuel," she said, "your papi won't be coming home for a while." She told us it was all right for us to cry, and she did too.

After that, Mama couldn't pick us up from school anymore because she had to get another job. We took the school bus home instead and couldn't play outside with our friends after school. Mama said we had to stay in the house and lock the door to make sure we were safe until she got home.

That was months ago. Now there are boxes
all over the house. We are moving. Mama
says she doesn't make enough money, even
with her second job, to pay for everything by
herself. The swing set Papi made for us has
to stay behind. He won't be here to push me
on the swing one last time before we leave.

We are going to move in with my tíos and cousins for a while.
It will be fun to share a bedroom with my cousin Malena.
But I am sad that I will have to change schools and say
goodbye to all my friends.

Mama says we are lucky. She met other moms
when she visited my dad who had no places for
their families to go when they had to move.

I get to stay on my soccer team,
but it feels different now that Papi
isn't our coach anymore.

I miss hearing him cheer and laugh
when we score a goal.

Last week was my birthday.
I was ten years old. Friends came
to our house, and we had balloons
and cake and presents and even
a bouncy house.

But Papi wasn't there to pull the rope for
the piñata up and down as we tried to hit it,
so it wasn't the same.

A mean boy at school said, "They took your dad
away because he did something bad." It made me
feel sad and mad at the same time. Mama says Papi
never did anything wrong; he just didn't have papers.
I don't understand why they would send him so
far away because of some papers.

I got scared and asked if they could take her away too or even me and my brother. She said my brother and I were safe because we were born here, and that she had a special card that kept her safe. I wish they'd give Papi a card so he could be safe with us too.

They have kept Papi in a place far away from
us for a long time. He said it wasn't a good place for
children to see, so Mama goes by herself on a bus to visit him.

Even though it wasn't
Valentine's Day, I cut a heart
out of red paper and wrote
"I love you, Papi" on it for
Mama to give to him.

Papi writes me little notes that come in the mail with letters to Mama. It is exciting to get my own mail, but I would rather have my dad here instead. I keep all the notes in a jewelry box I got for my birthday. When I miss Papi a lot, I take them out and read them again and again.

Mama says they will be sending Papi to live in
another country very soon. I am scared, because
I heard her and my aunt talking about how they
left that country because it was too dangerous.

My stomach has been hurting a lot lately. The doctor said I wasn't really sick. He said it was because of all the changes and from missing my dad so much. Mama is worried about me. But how can I stop missing my dad?

She tells me love is like the orange moon, that Papi and I feel its glow no matter where we are.

The orange moon is high
in the night sky now.

I wonder if Papi is thinking about me too,
under the same mango moon.

*To all the families who
suffer forced separation, whose
love reaches beyond borders*
—DdA

*For my grandson,
Ezra Zen, with love*
—SC

Library of Congress Cataloging-in-Publication data is on file with the publisher.

Text copyright © 2019 by Diane de Anda
Illustrations copyright © 2019 by Sue Cornelison
First published in the United States of America in 2019 by Albert Whitman & Company
ISBN 978-0-8075-4957-5

Printed in China
10 9 8 7 6 5 4 3 2 1 WKT 22 21 20 19 18

Design by Aphee Messer

For more information about Albert Whitman & Company,
visit our website at www.albertwhitman.com.

100 Years of Albert Whitman & Company
Celebrate with us in 2019!